The Jungle Book

A DK Publishing Book

www.dk.com

Project Editor Rebecca Smith
Art Editor Tanya Tween
Senior Editor Marie Greenwood
Managing Art Editor Jacquie Gulliver
Picture Research Andrea Sadler and Cynthia Frazer
DTP Designer Jill Bunyan
Production Joanne Rooke

First American Edition, 1999

2 4 6 8 10 9 7 5 3 1

Published in the United States by
DK Publishing, Inc.
95 Madison Avenue
New York, New York 10016

Grindley, Sally.
 The jungle book/by Rudyard Kipling; adapted by Sally Grindley;
illustrated by Julek Heller. -- 1st American ed.
  p. cm. -- (Young Classics)
Summary: A simplified retelling of the adventures of Mowgli, a
young boy raised by the animals in an Indian jungle, as well as
other animal stories.
 ISBN 0-7894-4944-7
1. Children's stories, English. [1. Jungles Fiction. 2. Animals Fiction.
3. India Fiction. 4. Short stories.] I. Heller, Julek,
ill. II. Kipling, Rudyard, 1865–1936. Jungle book. III. Title.
IV. Series.
PZ7.G88446Ju 1999
[Fic]--dc21   99-33391
                                                        CIP

Color reproduction by Bright Arts, Hong Kong
Printed in Italy by L.E.G.O.

Acknowledgments
The publisher would like to thank the following for their kind permission to reproduce their photographs:

a=above; c=center; b=bottom/below; l=left; r=right; t=top
AA Photolibrary: 7 cl; **Bridgeman Art Library, London/New York:** 6 cra; Chris Beetles Ltd. London, UK 47 cr; **British Museum, London:** 42 cr; **Corbis UK Ltd:** 48 tl; **Douglas Dickens:** 24 tl; **Dinodia Picture Agency:** V. I. Thayil 6 clb; **E.T. Archive:** 48 crb, 48 montage; **Mary Evans Picture Library:** 46 bc; **Fotomas Index:** 46 clb; **Robert Harding Syndication/IPC Magazines Ltd:** 29 tr, Duncan Maxwell 34 cl; **Hulton Getty:** 7 tr; **Kobal Collection:** The Walt Disney Company 47 tl; **London Library:** J. Lockwood Kipling 46 cr; **National Gallery, London:** 4; **National Trust Photographic Library:** Geoffrey Frosh 48 bl, John Hammond 48 cr, 48 cl; **N.H.P.A:** E. Hanumantha Rao 7 br, 7 bl, 22 bl, 39 tr; K. Ghani 44 cr; Morten Strange 7 clb; **Planet Earth Pictures:** Anup and Mandj Shah 8 b; Georgette Douwma 36 clb; Tom Walker 6 bc, 15 tr.
Jacket: **Corbis UK Ltd:** inside back flap; **Robert Harding Syndication/IPC Magazines Ltd:** Duncan Maxwell Back cr; **N.H.P.A:** Morten Strange inside front flap.

Dorling Kindersley would like to thank:
John Woodcock (additional illustration), Alastair Dougall,
and Jacky Jackson (editorial assistance), and Laia Roses
and Lisa Lanzarini (design assistance).

YOUNG DK CLASSICS

The Jungle Book

By **Rudyard Kipling**
Retold by **Sally Grindley**

Illustrated by
Julek Heller

DK Publishing, Inc.

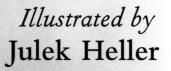

Tiger in a Tropical Storm, *Henri Rousseau, 1891*

Contents

Kipling's India

RUDYARD KIPLING'S stories about Mowgli the man–cub are set in central India in the late 19th century. Kipling was born in India and spent his early life there. His father had explored the jungles of central India, and the stories he told inspired Kipling to create a jungle world all of his own.

✳ THE BRITISH IN INDIA

The India Kipling knew as a child was under British rule and had been since the 18th century. Kipling's family was one of many British families that chose to live and work in India.

✳ THE JUNGLE SETTING

Kipling set his jungle stories in the Seoni hills of central India. This area is covered with dense forests and rocky hills and has many rivers and streams running through it. The region is now a national park and a tiger reserve.

Bagheera (Bug-eer-a) comes from the word for jungle cat in many Indian languages.

✳ CALL OF THE WILD

India is home to hundreds of wild animals and birds, many of which can be found in *The Jungle Book*. Many of the names Kipling gave to the animals originated from local dialects that Kipling knew.

The word "shere" in the name Shere Khan (Sheer Kaan) means "tiger."

Baloo (Bah-loo) is an Indian word for bear.

☀ THE LAND OF INDIA

India has a varied landscape. There are mountains in the north, dry desert areas to the west, and also forests and jungles. Many rivers run through India – the name "India" comes from the River Indus – and the fertile land is used to grow crops such as rice, wheat, and tea.

Kipling lived in this house in Lahore (now in Pakistan, which was made a separate country in 1947).

LAHORE

DELHI

INDIA

GANGES

DHAKA

CHITTOR

SEONI

WAINGANGA

CALCUTTA

NARMADA

BOMBAY

GODAVARI

KRISHNA

MADRAS

Kipling visited the ruined temples of Chittor and was so impressed that he set one of his chapters in an imaginary ruined city called "Cold Lairs."

Kipling set his book around the Wainganga River, which runs near the Seoni hills.

Chil (Cheel) comes from the sound the kite makes.

Jackals like Tabaqui (Tabahky) feed on the kill of other animals.

Kipling explains that Akela (Uk-kay-la) means "alone." In the story, Akela is the Lone Wolf.

Pythons like Kaa (Kah) can swallow small animals whole!

The name Bandarlog (Bunder-log) comes from an Indian word for Bengal monkey.

Mowgli's Brothers

ONE WARM EVENING, in a cave in the Seoni hills of India, Father Wolf woke from his day's rest. Mother Wolf lay beside him, her long gray nose resting gently across her four squealing cubs.

"Ah well, time to hunt again," said Father Wolf, stretching his legs. But as he prepared to spring down the hill, a shadow fell across the opening of the cave.

"Spare a thought, O Noble Wolf, for the hungry of this world." It was Tabaqui, the Jackal, who was hated by the wolves because he told tales and scrounged for food, but was feared too because of his violent temper.

"You won't find any food here," said Father Wolf stiffly.

"I see a dry bone," said Tabaqui, scuttling to the back of the cave. He sat chewing the bone, pleased to be able to make Father Wolf wait. Then he said spitefully, "My tiger friend, Shere Khan, will be hunting among these hills, so he tells me."

"He has no right!" cried Father Wolf, angrily. "He can't just change hunting grounds without warning."

"He is lame in one foot and can only kill cattle," said Mother Wolf. "Once he attacks the cattle here, the villagers will search through our forests and set fire to the grass all around us to catch him. How good of him to bring us such trouble!"

Jackals survive on the scraps of food left by other animals. This has led to their reputation as wily, scavenging creatures.

"Shall I tell him how pleased you are?" said Tabaqui.

"Out!" snapped Father Wolf. "You've done enough harm for one night."

"I will go," said Tabaqui quietly.

"You can hear Shere Khan below in the thickets. I might have saved myself the message."

From down in the valley echoed the dry, angry, snarly, sing-song whine of a tiger who has failed to make a catch.

"With that noise he'll frighten away every deer within miles," said Father Wolf.

"Hush," said Mother Wolf. The whine had changed to a sort of loud humming purr. "He's not hunting cattle or deer right now. He's hunting Man."

The purr grew louder and was followed by a mighty "Aaarh!" as the tiger charged. Then there was a strange howl. Father Wolf took a few steps outside and heard Shere Khan muttering furiously as he thrashed around in the undergrowth.

"The idiot has burned his feet on a woodcutter's fire," grunted Father Wolf.

"Something's coming up the hill," said Mother Wolf.

Father Wolf crouched down ready to pounce, pushed off from the ground, and then twisted around in mid-air to land back where he had started.

"Man!" he cried. *"Out!" snapped*
"A man's cub. Look!" *Father Wolf.*

There, holding
shakily onto a low
branch, stood a naked,
brown baby boy. He gazed
into Father Wolf's face and
gurgled happily.

"Is that a man's cub?"
asked Mother Wolf. "I've
never seen one. Bring it here."

Father Wolf picked up the baby, O so gently
in his teeth, and laid him down among his cubs.

"He's so tiny," whispered Mother Wolf, "yet look how boldly
he's pushing his way through our cubs to feed."

At that moment, the cave grew dark. Shere Khan's great
square head filled the entrance. Behind him, Tabaqui squawked,
"My lord, it went in here."

"We are honored by your visit," said Father Wolf steadily, but his
eyes were full of anger. "What can we do for you?"

"A man's cub went this way," growled Shere Khan. "Give it to me."

"We wolves are free people," said Father Wolf. "We take our
orders from the head of our Pack, not from a lame cattle killer."

"How dare you defy me? It is I, Shere Khan, who speak!"

His roar filled the cave.
Mother Wolf freed herself
from her cubs and sprang
forward, her eyes, like two
green moons in the
darkness, facing the blazing
eyes of Shere Khan.

"And it is I, Raksha,

*Tigers are renowned for
their fierce natures. Hunting
alone, they usually choose
deer or cattle for food.
But old or injured tigers,
like Shere Khan,
sometimes attack people.*

who answer.
The man's cub
is mine. He shall
not be killed. He
will live to run
and hunt with the
Pack. And in the
end – be warned,
you coward – he will
hunt you. Now go, or
I will see to it that you
are unable to walk at all."

Shere Khan knew
that Mother Wolf would
fight to the death. He
backed out of the cave-
mouth, but as he turned
to go he roared, "It is
easy to sound brave from
the safety of your cave. We
shall see what the Pack thinks
about you raising man-cubs. That cub
is mine and I shall have him."

Father Wolf turned to Mother Wolf
and said, "Shere Khan is right. The man-cub must be
shown to the Pack. Do you still want to keep him?"

*Shere Khan's great square
head filled the entrance.*

"Keep him!" she gasped. "I most certainly will.
I will call him Mowgli the frog. Lie still, little frog. One day, you will
hunt down Shere Khan, just as he has hunted you."

"But what will our Pack say?" said Father Wolf anxiously.

Father Wolf was bound by the Law of the Jungle to introduce his cubs to the Pack as soon as they could stand. Now, on the night of the Pack meeting, he led them to Council Rock – a hilltop covered with large boulders where a hundred wolves could hide. Akela, the Pack leader, lay stretched out on his rock, which overlooked a circle of some forty wolves whose cubs romped in the center. Every so often he cried: "You know the Law. Look well, O Wolves!"
The wolves would then look carefully at each of the cubs, in order to recognize them. They would not be forgiven for harming a cub belonging to their own Pack.

Father and Mother Wolf exchanged worried glances and pushed Mowgli forward. Just then, an angry roar came from behind a rock and Shere Khan snarled: "That cub is mine. Give him to me. What have the Free People to do with a man's cub?"

Some of the wolves growled in agreement: "What have the Free People to do with a man's cub?"

At that Akela cried: "Who among the Free People will speak for this cub, apart from his father and mother?"

None of the wolves answered, and Mother Wolf prepared for a fight. Then the only other creature who was allowed at the Pack Council –

Baloo, the sleepy Brown Bear – rose up and grunted.

"I speak for the man's cub. There is no harm in a man's cub. Let him run with the Pack. I will teach him the Law of the Jungle."

"We need another," said Akela. "Who else speaks for the man's cub?"

A black shadow dropped down into the circle. It was Bagheera, the Black Panther. "O Akela," he purred, his voice as soft as wild honey dripping from a tree. "I have no right to be at your meeting, yet the Law says that anyone may buy the life of a cub, at a price. I will offer one fat bull, newly killed, if you will accept the man's cub into the Pack."

Immediately, dozens of hungry voices cried: "What harm can a man's cub do us?"

Akela cried again: "Look well, O Wolves!" The wolves studied Mowgli carefully, then rushed down the hill to feast on the dead bull. But Shere Khan roared with anger into the night. ✳

"Look well, O Wolves!"

The Monkey People

BALOO WAS DELIGHTED with his new pupil. He taught Mowgli how to tell a rotten branch from a sturdy one; how to speak politely to bees; what to say to Mang the bat if he disturbed him during the day; how to warn water snakes before he dived down among them. Sometimes, Bagheera would lounge through the jungle to see how his pet was getting on.

"How can his little head carry all of this?" he said to Baloo, after Baloo had bellowed at Mowgli and Mowgli had run off in a temper.

"He's not too little to be killed," said Baloo. "That's why I raise my voice a little when he forgets."

"A little!" said Bagheera. "His ears are ringing with your roaring."

"Would you rather he came to harm because of something he doesn't know?" argued Baloo. "I am now teaching him the Master Words of the Jungle. If he can only remember them, they will protect him from everything in the jungle."

"So," said Bagheera, "just what are those Master Words?"

"I'll call Mowgli, and he can tell you. Come, little brother," called Baloo.

"My ears are ringing like a bee tree," came a sullen voice from above. Mowgli slid down a tree trunk and added: "I'm coming for Bagheera, not you, fat old Baloo."

"That's all the same to me," said Baloo,

Mowgli jumped on Bagheera's back.

though he was hurt. "Tell Bagheera, then, the Master Words for creatures that hunt."

"*We are of one blood, you and I,*" said Mowgli. Then he continued with the Master Words for birds, and snakes. When he had finished, he jumped on Bagheera's back, and made the worst faces he could think of at Baloo.

"It was worth a little scolding," Baloo said tenderly. "Now, Mowgli has no one to fear."

A big bear like Baloo is able to look after himself. But Mowgli must learn all the animal languages – the "Master Words" – in order to survive.

"Except his own Pack," muttered Bagheera.

"I'll soon have a tribe of my own and lead them through the branches all day long," shouted Mowgli suddenly at the top of his voice. "They have promised me."

WHOOF! Baloo's big paw scooped Mowgli off Bagheera's back. "You've been talking to the Monkey People," he said angrily.

"They were kind to me when you shouted at me," snuffled Mowgli. "They said I could be their leader."

"They have no leader," said Bagheera. "They lie."

"Why haven't you ever taken me to the Monkey People, when they stand on two feet just like I do."

"Listen, man-cub," said Baloo. "I have taught you the Law of the Jungle for all the creatures of the jungle, except the Monkey People. They have no law. The Jungle People are forbidden to go near them."

As he spoke a shower of nuts spattered down through the branches and they could hear angry howlings from high above. "Come now," said Bagheera. "It's time for our midday nap."

The next thing
Mowgli knew, he was hanging
upside down with the earth a long way
below. Baloo's deep cries woke the jungle,
while Bagheera bounded up a trunk and bared his
teeth. The monkeys howled triumphantly: "He has
noticed us! Bagheera has noticed us!" Then, bounding
and crashing and whooping and yelling, the whole tribe
swept off through the jungle, carrying Mowgli between them.
Mowgli could not help enjoying the wild flight, though glimpses
of the earth far down below frightened him. His escorts would rush
him up a tree till he felt the top most branches crackle and bend
under their weight. Then with a cough and a whoop they would
fling themselves into the air and land, hanging by their hands or
feet, on the lower limbs of the next tree. Sometimes Mowgli could
see for miles and miles across the still green roof of the jungle, and
then the branches and leaves would lash him across the face and he
would be almost down to earth again.

For a time, Mowgli was afraid of being dropped. Then he grew
angry. Then he began to think. The first thing he had to do was
somehow send word back to Baloo and Bagheera of his
whereabouts. He knew that by now they would be far behind.
There was no point in looking down because all he could see were
the topsides of the branches. So he stared upward. High up in the
sky he saw Chil the kite hovering over the jungle, searching for
food. Chil saw that the monkeys were carrying something, and
dropped down to find out what it was. He whistled with
surprise when he saw a man-cub being dragged through the
trees and heard him give the kite call for – "*We are of one
blood, you and I.*" Mowgli disappeared from sight beneath

*"Mark my trail!" Mowgli
shouted to Chil the Kite.*

the waves of branches. Chil
hovered overhead and waited for
him to come up again. "Mark my
trail," Mowgli shouted. "Tell Baloo and
Bagheera where I am."

"Who shall I say you are, Brother?"
Chil had never seen Mowgli before,
though he had heard of him.

"Mowgli, the frog. Man-cub
they call me! Mark my tra-il!"
The last words were shrieked as
he was swung roughly through
the air, but Chil nodded and rose
up toward the clouds.

"They won't go far,"
he chuckled.

"The Monkey People
never do what they set out to
do. They are always pecking at
new things. Well, this time they've
pecked a lot of trouble for
themselves, for Baloo is no fool and
Bagheera can kill more than just
goats." So he hovered overhead,
and waited.

Agile and strong, black panthers like Bagheera often spring up trees to catch their prey. But Bagheera's strength cannot rescue Mowgli from the monkeys – he must use cunning instead.

Meanwhile, Baloo and Bagheera were furious with rage and grief.

"Why didn't you warn Mowgli about the Monkey People?" Bagheera roared.

"Quick! We might still catch them," panted Baloo.

"At that speed you couldn't catch a wounded cow! And they may drop him if we follow too close."

"Arrula! Whoo! They may have dropped him already!" howled Baloo. "Roll me into the hives of wild bees, for I am the most miserable of bears!" Baloo clasped his paws over his ears and rolled on the ground moaning.

"At least he recited the Master Words of the Jungle correctly," said Bagheera impatiently. "But he is in the power of the Monkey People, the 'Bandarlog,' and they are not afraid of us."

"They're afraid of Kaa the Python," said Baloo, sitting up with a jerk. "He steals young monkeys. Let's go to Kaa for help."

"Pah! Why should that footless, evil-eyed old devil help us?"

"Promise him food and he might," said Baloo eagerly. "Together we could persuade him." He rubbed shoulders with Bagheera, and they went off in search of Kaa.

They found him stretched out on a ledge, admiring his new skin and twisting the thirty feet of his body into knots and curves.

"Oho, Baloo, Bagheera, what are you doing here?"

"We are hunting," said Baloo casually.

"O, let me come with you, I am as empty as a dried well," said Kaa. "I nearly fell on my last hunt. The noise of my slipping woke the Bandarlog and they called me all sorts of nasty names."

"Like 'footless, yellow earthworm'?"

asked Bagheera cunningly. "They say that you've lost all your teeth and won't hunt anything bigger than a baby goat."

Kaa rarely showed that he was angry, but Baloo and Bagheera could see the big swallowing muscles on either side of his throat ripple and bulge.

"Those nut-stealers have run off with our man-cub," said Bagheera.

"The finest man-cub that ever was," said Baloo.

"Of all the Jungle People, the Bandarlog fear Kaa alone," said Bagheera quickly.

"So, where did they go?" asked Kaa.

But they were interrupted by a shrill, "Look up!"

Above them was Chil.

"What are you doing?" asked Kaa.

"I have seen Mowgli. He spoke the Master Words and begged me to tell you his whereabouts. They have taken him to the monkey city, Cold Lairs."

"To think of one so young remembering the Master Words for the birds while being dragged through the treetops," said Baloo, chuckling with pride. ✳

Kaa's Hunting

COLD LAIRS was an old deserted city. Few of the Jungle People ever went there, for that is where the Monkey People – the Bandarlog – lived, if they could be said to live anywhere.

"It will take half the night to get there," said Bagheera. "We dare not wait for you, Baloo. Kaa and I must go as fast as we can."

Baloo attempted to keep up with them, but soon had to sit down panting. Bagheera darted forward at a canter, while Kaa seemed to pour himself along the ground, seeking out the shortest route with his steady eyes.

"You're certainly not slow," said Bagheera.

"I'm hungry," said Kaa. "Besides, they called me speckled frog."

Meanwhile, Mowgli sat miserably in Cold Lairs, watching the monkeys dancing and singing foolish songs. "You could at least bring me some food," he said crossly. Dozens of monkeys bounded away to pick him some nuts and fruit, but they began fighting and couldn't be bothered to go back with the mess that was left.

So Mowgli set off to explore. He had never seen a city before, and even though this one was in ruins it seemed very wonderful. He followed the paths that led to the ruined gates. Trees had pushed through the walls and creepers hung out of the windows of the towers. A great roofless palace crowned the hill, and the cobblestones in the courtyard had been thrust up by grasses and young trees. From the palace Mowgli looked out across rows of roofless houses and the shattered domes of temples.

The Bandarlog called the place their city and despised the Jungle People for living in the forest. But they hadn't the slightest clue

how to live
properly in such a place.
They would sit in circles
scratching for fleas and pretending
to be men. They would gather in great
crowds and fight, or they would rush
together in mobs and shout.

Mowgli did not like or understand this
kind of life and felt he had come to a very
bad place indeed. "All that Baloo has said
about the Bandarlog is true," he thought to
himself. "I must try to get out of here. I'd rather
have Baloo bellow at me."

But when he reached the city walls, the
monkeys pulled him back and took him
to a ruined summerhouse. Hundreds of
them gathered on the terraces to listen
to their leaders. "We are great. We are
free. We are the most wonderful
people in all the jungle! We all say
so, so it must be true,"
they shouted.

Mowgli felt he had come to
a very bad place indeed.

"You can carry our words back to the Jungle People so that they will notice us in future," they told Mowgli.

Little did the Bandarlog know that Bagheera and Kaa were watching them from the ruined ditch below the city wall. "I'll go to the west wall," whispered Kaa, "and glide swiftly down the slope toward them. They won't jump on me, however many there are of them."

"I still wish Baloo were here to help," said Bagheera. "We'll have to do what we can."

The monkeys turned on Bagheera.

"Good hunting," said Kaa grimly and slithered away.

As soon as a cloud covered the moon, Bagheera raced up to the terrace where Mowgli was captive. He struck out at the monkeys, who were crowded round Mowgli. There were howls of fright, then a monkey shrieked: "There is only one of them! Kill him!" The monkeys turned on Bagheera and, biting and scratching, piled on top of him. Others grabbed Mowgli, dragged him up the wall of the summerhouse, and pushed him through a hole in the broken dome. "Stay there until we have killed your friend," shouted the monkeys, "then we'll play with you – if the Poison People don't kill you first."

Monkeys are found in ruined cities all over India. In large groups they are often very noisy and can be aggressive, as Bagheera discovers.

Mowgli heard a sinister hissing from the piles of garbage. "*We are of one blood, you and I*," he said, giving the Snake's Call.

"Stand still then, Little Brother, or you'll tread on us," came the reply.

Mowgli stood still and listened anxiously to the furious screams coming from up above as Bagheera fought for his life.

"Baloo must be close by," thought Mowgli. "Bagheera would never have come on his own." He called out loud: "Run to the water, Bagheera. Get to the water."

Hearing Mowgli's voice gave Bagheera new courage. He began to crawl his way slowly, desperately toward the reservoirs.

And then Baloo's rumbling war cry rose up from one of the ruined walls. "Ahuwora! Bagheera, I'm here now! I'm coming to get you, you wicked Bandarlog."

He panted up the terrace on all fours and was immediately overrun by monkeys. But he pulled himself up on his haunches and grabbed as many of them as he could in a tight bear hug. Then he spread out his front paws and began to hit them with a regular bat-bat-bat, like the flipping strokes of a paddle wheel.

Mowgli heard a loud splash and knew that Bagheera had reached the reservoir. The Black Panther lay, head above the water, gasping for breath. In despair, he gave the Snake's Call for help — "*We are of one blood, you and I*" — for he was sure that Kaa had fled.

Baloo grabbed as many monkeys as he could.

Kipling based Cold Lairs on the ruined cities he visited. The temples and palaces, abandoned by men, soon became homes for monkeys and snakes.

Kaa had slid over the west wall and landed badly. While he stopped to check that every coil of his body was in working order, the fight with Baloo raged on. Gangs of monkeys came from far and wide to help their comrades in the Cold Lairs.

At last, Kaa's thirty feet of snaking power sped down to the battleground. His first whopping blow was delivered into the heart of the crowd around Baloo. As soon as they saw him, the monkeys scattered with cries of "Kaa! It's Kaa! Run!"

Kaa was everything the Bandarlog feared. None of them knew the limits of his power, none of them could look into his dazzling eyes, and no monkey had ever come out alive from his hug. And so they fled in terror. Then Kaa spoke one long, hissing word. At once, the monkeys on the walls and roofs of the city stopped their cries. Even the far away monkeys cowered in the treetops. During the silence that fell, Bagheera crawled out of the reservoir.

"Did I hear you call for me?" said Kaa.

"I – I might have cried out in the battle," Bagheera said quietly, then turned quickly to Baloo who was exploring his wounds. "Are you hurt, my friend?"

"I feel as though I've been pulled into a hundred little bearlings," said Baloo. "Kaa, we owe you our lives, Bagheera and I."

"It's nothing," said Kaa. "Where is the manling?"

"I'm down here," yelled Mowgli. "I can't climb out."

Kaa looked carefully for a weak point in the wall of the summerhouse, then, lifting six feet of his body from the ground, he smashed into it nose-first. The wall fell away in a pile of dust, and Mowgli leaped through the opening. He ran between Baloo and Bagheera and flung his arms around their necks.

"Are you hurt?' said Baloo, hugging him gently.

"Sore, hungry, and bruised," said Mowgli. "But you are bleeding!"

"As long as you're safe that's all that matters," whimpered Baloo.

"We'll see about that later," said Bagheera dryly. "But now you must thank Kaa, according to our customs, for saving your life."

"So this is the manling," said Kaa. "His skin is soft and he looks a little like the Bandarlog. Take care I don't mistake you for a monkey."

"*We are of one blood, you and I,*" said Mowgli quickly. "You saved my life tonight. Anything I kill will be yours to share if ever you are hungry, Brother Kaa."

"Thanks, Little Brother," said Kaa with a twinkle in his eyes. "But now you must leave quickly with your friends. The moon is setting and you should not watch what is about to happen."

The wall fell away in a pile of dust.

As the moon sank down, Kaa glided to the center of the terrace and snapped his jaws together. The lines of trembling monkeys turned their eyes on him.

"The moon is setting," he said. "Can you still see?" From the walls came a moan like the wind in the treetops – "We see, O Kaa."

"Then sit and watch my dance – the Dance of the Hunger of Kaa." Kaa turned in a big circle, weaving his head from left to right and humming softly. Then he began making loops and figures of eight, and triangles that melted into squares, never resting, never hurrying, and humming all the time. It grew darker and darker until nothing could be seen and only the rustle of his scales could be heard.

"Sit and watch my dance."

Baloo and Bagheera stood as still as statues, while Mowgli watched and wondered.

"Bandarlog," said Kaa at last. "Can you move without my order?"

"Without your order we cannot move hand or foot, O Kaa!"

"Good! Then come one step closer to me."

The monkeys swayed forward helplessly. Baloo and Bagheera stepped forward with them.

"Closer!" hissed Kaa, and they all moved again.

Mowgli laid his hands on Baloo and Bagheera. They jumped as though they had been woken from a dream.

Pythons kill their prey by crushing them in their coils. They then swallow the creature whole. Kaa uses another tactic with the monkeys – he hypnotizes them first.

"Keep your hand on my shoulder," Bagheera whispered. "Keep it there or I will go back to Kaa."

"It's only that silly old snake making circles in the dust," said Mowgli, as the three of them slipped through a gap in the walls into the jungle.

"Whoof!" said Baloo as he shook himself all over. "I don't think I want to get too close to Kaa again."

"If we'd stayed, I would have walked down his throat," said Bagheera, trembling.

"Many will walk down that road before the moon rises again," said Baloo. "He will have good hunting."

"But what did it all mean?" said Mowgli. "All I saw was a snake going around and around in circles. And his nose was sore. Tee-hee!"

"Mowgli," said Bagheera angrily, "his nose is sore because of you. Just as Baloo and I are sore because of you. Don't forget that I, the Black Panther, was forced to ask Kaa for help, and Baloo and I were both made to look foolish by his Hunger Dance. All because you played with the Bandarlog. Now, according to the Law of the Jungle, you must be punished."

"I am a bad man-cub," said Mowgli, sorrowfully.

"Be gentle with him," said Baloo. "He is only little."

Bagheera gave Mowgli a dozen love taps. To Mowgli they felt like a severe beating, but when it was over he picked himself up without a word. "Now," said Bagheera, "jump on my back, Little Brother, and we'll go home." ✷

Red Flower

MOWGLI LED A WONDERFUL LIFE among the wolves and with his friends, Baloo and Bagheera. When he wasn't learning the meaning of things in the jungle from Father Wolf or Baloo, what he loved most was to go with Bagheera into the heart of the forest and watch him hunting. By night, he would go down the hillside to the village and gaze curiously at the villagers in their huts.

But over everything hung the threat of Shere Khan. As Akela grew older and began to lose control of the Pack, Shere Khan spent more and more time with the younger wolves. He would call them fine hunters and ask why they were happy to be led by a dying wolf and a man's cub. When he mocked them for not daring to look Mowgli in the eyes, the wolves would growl and bristle.

Over everything hung the threat of Shere Khan.

Bagheera told Mowgli that one day Shere Khan would kill him, but Mowgli laughed: "I have the Pack, and I have you and Baloo. Shere Khan is all long tail and loud talk. Why should I be afraid?"

"The younger wolves have been taught by Shere Khan that a man-cub has no place with the Pack," said Bagheera. "When Akela misses his next kill, the Pack will turn against him, and you."

"But they're my brothers," said Mowgli. "Why would they want to kill me?"

"Look at me," said Bagheera. Mowgli looked at him steadily. The big panther turned his head away in half a minute. "That is why," said

Bagheera. "Even I cannot look at you between the eyes, and I love you, Little Brother. The others hate you because they cannot look you in the eye, because you are wiser

Fire is an essential part of village life. It provides warmth and protection. But for the jungle animals, fire is a sign of danger and destruction.

than they are, you can do things they can't – because you are a man."

Suddenly, Bagheera leapt to his feet. "I have an idea. Go down to the men's huts in the valley and take some of the Red Flower that grows there in little pots. With that by your side, no jungle creature will come near you."

Mowgli set off swiftly through the forest, plunging down through the bushes to the stream at the bottom of the valley. He heard the Pack hunting and the young wolves howling: "Akela! Akela! Let the Lone Wolf show his strength." He dashed on, knowing that Bagheera had told him the truth.

When he reached the village, he peered through the window of a hut and saw a fire burning in the hearth. By first light of morning, the fire had died down, and Mowgli saw a young boy fill a small pot with lumps of red-hot charcoal and carry it outside. Mowgli ran around the hut, took the pot from the boy's hands and disappeared back into the forest. Halfway up the hill, Mowgli met Bagheera.

"Akela has missed," said Bagheera. "They would have killed him already, but they want you as well."

"I am ready for them," said Mowgli.

———— ·◆· ————

"I am ready," said Mowgli.

That very evening, Tabaqui the Jackal came to tell Mowgli that he was wanted at the Council Rock. Mowgli picked up the fire-pot and a branch, and made his way, laughing, to the Council.

Akela lay by the side of his rock to show that he was no longer leader, while Shere Khan sauntered to and fro being flattered by his young supporters. Bagheera drew close to Mowgli, who sat down with the fire-pot between his knees.

Shere Khan rose to his feet. "Since the leadership is open, and I have been asked to speak —" he began.

"Who asked you?" interrupted Mowgli. "Are we all such jackals that we have to lick the feet of a cattle butcher? The leadership is the Pack's affair, and it is up to the Pack alone to sort it out."

The young wolves all yelled, "Silence, man-cub. The tiger has kept our Law, so let him speak." But the older members of the Pack thundered: "Let Akela speak."

Akela raised his old head wearily. "Free People," he began. "For twelve seasons I have led you to and from the kill, and in that time no one has been trapped or injured. Now I have missed my kill, though some of you plotted cleverly to make that happen.

Nevertheless, it is your right to kill me here and now. So, I ask, who will be first to finish me off? For it is my right that you must take me on one by one."

"Let the man-cub go," said Akela.

There was a long silence. No single wolf cared to fight Akela to the death. Then Shere Khan roared: "Bah, who cares about this toothless old fool? He is doomed to die. It is the man-cub who has lived too long. Give him to me."

At once, more than half the Pack began to yell: "What has a man to do with us? Let him go to his own place."

"No, give him to me," roared Shere Khan. "If we let him go he will turn all the villages against us."

Akela lifted his head again, and said: "He has eaten our food, slept among us, and helped us hunt. He is our brother in all but blood."

"No man's cub can run with the people of the jungle," howled Shere Khan. "Give him to me!"

"For the sake of the honor of the Pack," continued Akela, "I promise that if you let the man-cub go, I will die without fighting. At least I can save you from the shame that comes from killing a blameless brother, a brother spoken for and brought into the Pack according to the Law of the Jungle."

"He is a man – a man – a man!" snarled the pack, as they gathered around Shere Khan.

"Now it's up to you," whispered Bagheera to Mowgli. "All we can do is fight."

*Mowgli grabbed the tiger by
the tuft of the chin.*

Mowgli leapt to his feet, the fire-pot in his hands. He was furious with rage and sorrow, for he had never realized how much the wolves hated him. "Listen," he cried. "You have told me so many times tonight that I am a man – even though I have lived my whole life with you as a wolf – that what you say must be true. So I will not call you my brothers any more, but 'dogs' just as a man would. And in case you want to argue the point, try arguing with this."

He hurled the fire-pot to the ground. Red coals spilled out and lit a tuft of dried moss. The Pack shrank back in terror before the dancing flames. Mowgli thrust his dead branch into the flames until the twigs lit and whirled it around among the whimpering wolves. He gazed at them steadily. "I will leave you then, dogs, to join my own people. The jungle is closed to me, and I must forget all the years we have spent together as brothers."

Mowgli kicked the fire with his foot so that sparks flew up and strode over to where Shere Khan sat blinking stupidly at the flames. "There is one debt I intend to pay before I go," he said, and he grabbed the tiger by the tuft of the chin. "Up, dog!" he cried. "Stand up when a man speaks to you or I will set light to your coat."

Shere Khan cringed as the burning branch came closer. "This cattle killer wants to kill me now because he couldn't when I was a cub. Instead I'll show him how a man beats a dog. Twitch one whisker and I'll ram the Red Flower down your throat!" Mowgli beat Shere Khan over the head with the branch till the tiger whined in an agony of fear.

"Pah! Go now singed jungle-puss!" cried Mowgli triumphantly. He turned to the wolves and said: "Remember that when I come back to the Council Rock as a man, it will be with Shere Khan's hide on my head. And listen well: Akela is free to leave this place and live as he pleases. You will not kill him, because I say so. Now go."

Mowgli struck out with the blazing branch, and the wolves ran off howling. Soon, the only ones left were Akela, Bagheera, and a few wolves that had been on Mowgli's side. In the quiet that followed, Mowgli caught his breath. Deep inside him, he felt the biggest hurt he had ever felt. Tears filled his eyes and ran down his face.

"What is it?" he wailed. "I don't want to leave the jungle, but what is happening to me? Am I dying, Bagheera?"

"No, Little Brother," said Bagheera, gently. "Those are tears, tears that only men use. Now I know you are no longer a man-cub. Let them fall, Mowgli."

For the first time in his life, Mowgli cried, and he cried as though his heart would break. And then, as dawn broke, he set off down the hillside alone to meet those mysterious things that are called men. ✳

For the first time in his life Mowgli cried.

Village Life

MOWGLI WANTED to leave his enemies far behind. He ran and ran for twenty miles along a valley until it opened out into a great plain where cattle and buffaloes grazed. At one end stood a little village, at the other the jungle swept down but stopped where the grazing grounds began.

Mowgli reached the village gate and sat down. Soon a crowd of a hundred or so gathered by the gate and stared and shouted and pointed at Mowgli.

"They have no manners," said Mowgli to himself. "Only the Bandarlog would behave like this."

"No need to be afraid," said the priest. "Look at the bite marks on his arms and legs. He's just a wolf-child who has run away from the jungle."

"Let me see him," said a woman, pushing through the crowd. "He is thinner, but he is very like my boy who was taken by the tiger."

Now Mowgli must be accepted by his own "pack" and learn about village law. Luckily, life in the jungle has made him a quick learner.

The priest said solemnly: "What the jungle has taken away, the jungle has sent back. Give the boy a home, Messua."

Messua led Mowgli to her hut, where she gave him a long drink and some bread. She gazed into his eyes hoping to see a sign that this really was her son.

Mowgli felt uncomfortable because he had never been under a roof before, but he saw that he could easily escape through the window. Then he scolded himself for not being able to understand what Messua was saying. "What's the good of a man if he can't understand man's talk?"

While Mowgli was in the jungle he had
learned to imitate many of the beasts. So now, as
soon as Messua pronounced a word, he copied it
almost perfectly. Before dark, he had learned the
names of many things in the hut.

*Messua gave Mowgli a long
drink and some bread.*

But when night came, Mowgli refused to sleep inside. He leaped
through the window and stretched himself out in some long grass.

As he closed his eyes, a soft gray nose poked him under the chin.

"Pooh!" said Gray Brother, the oldest of Mother Wolf's cubs. "You smell of woodsmoke and cattle, just like a man."

"Are you all all right?" asked Mowgli, hugging him.

"Shere Khan's coat is badly singed. He's gone to hunt far away until it grows back. When he returns he swears he'll drop your bones to the bottom of the Wainganga River."

"I have my own plans for him. Promise you will always bring me news, Gray Brother?"

"You won't forget you are a wolf?" said Gray Brother anxiously.

"Never," said Mowgli. "I will always love our own family, but I will never forget that I have been cast out of the Pack."

"You may yet be cast out of another pack," said Gray Brother. "Men are only men and they are not to be trusted."

Mowgli spent the next few months learning the ways of men. He had to wear clothes, which he hated; he had to learn about money, which he didn't understand; and about plowing, which he thought was a waste of time. The little children in the village made fun of him because he wouldn't join in their games and because sometimes he said words in a funny way.

Although Mowgli has learned to communicate with men, he is still happier in the company of animals. He does not understand that the villagers think buffalo herding is a lowly job.

Mowgli had no understanding of religion or class, and that got him into trouble with the priest and the village elders. Before very long, they decided that he should be put to work herding the buffaloes.

No one was more pleased than Mowgli to be made a servant of the village. To celebrate, he went to the village club, where a circle of men met under a great fig tree to tell tales of gods and men and ghosts.

Buldeo, the village hunter, told stories about the ways of jungle animals. Mowgli sat and listened, but as the stories became more and more amazing he had to hide his face, he was laughing so much. When Buldeo explained how the tiger that had taken Messua's son was a ghost-tiger, which limped because it had the soul of a lame thief, Mowgli could hold his tongue no longer.

"Are all your stories such cobwebs and moon-talk?" he cried. "That tiger limps because he was born lame."

Buldeo was speechless with surprise at being interrupted by a child. Then he said: "Oh, it's the jungle brat, is it? If you're so wise, you'd better take the tiger's hide to the police, who are offering a hundred rupees for his life. Better still, don't interrupt your elders."

Mowgli leapt to his feet, and as he left he called back: "All evening I have sat here listening, and Buldeo has scarcely spoken one word of truth about the jungle." ☀

"Buldeo has scarcely spoken one word of truth about the jungle," Mowgli called out.

Tiger, Tiger!

AT DAWN the next day, Mowgli rode down the village street on the back of Rama, the great bull buffalo and leader of the herd. One by one, the other buffaloes left their stalls and followed him. Mowgli told the children with him that he was in charge, and sent them off to graze the cattle while he went on with the buffaloes. He drove the buffaloes to the edge of the plain, then dropped from Rama's neck and ran over to a clump of bamboo where Gray Brother was hiding.

"Shere Khan has been looking for you," said Gray Brother. "He's gone off again because there's too little for him to hunt here. But he means to kill you."

"While he's away," said Mowgli, "wait on that rock so that I can see you when I come out of the village. But when he comes back, wait for me by the orange-flowered tree in the middle of the plain, and then I will know."

With that, Mowgli found a shady spot and lay down and slept while the buffaloes grazed all around him.

Day after day, as Mowgli left the village he could see Gray

Brother perched on the rock. Safe in the knowledge that Shere Khan had not returned, he would lie down in the grass and dream about his old life in the jungle.

Wolves are renowned for hunting together in packs. Mowgli understands how to work with the wolves and can use their skills to trap Shere Khan.

But the day came when Gray Brother wasn't there. Mowgli herded the buffaloes toward the center of the plains and found Gray Brother by the tree.

"Shere Khan will be waiting for you at the village gate this evening."

"Has he eaten today?" asked Mowgli, knowing that a hungry tiger was far more dangerous than one that had recently fed.

"He killed a pig at dawn, now he's resting in the deep ravine by the river."

"Does he think I'm going to wait until he has slept it off?" laughed Mowgli.

"Shere Khan is waiting for you," said Gray Brother.

"That ravine opens out onto the plain only half a mile from here. I could take the herd around through the jungle to the head of the ravine and then charge down - but he could escape from the other end. How can we block it? Gray Brother, can you divide the herd in two?"

"I can't," said Gray Brother, "but Akela can."

From a hole nearby, Akela's great head appeared.

"Akela!" cried Mowgli. "I knew you wouldn't forget me. I need your help. Can you cut the herd in two, keeping the cows and calves away from the bulls?"

Akela nodded and the two wolves set to work, running in and out of the herd until it was separated into two snorting, stamping, pawing clumps. Mowgli leapt onto Rama's back and, with Akela's help, began to lead the bulls away to the left. Gray Brother held the cows together and drove them into the foot of the ravine.

Mowgli took the bulls in a long circle uphill through the jungle until he reached the head of the ravine. There he rounded them up and gave them time to regain their breath. Then he put his hands around his mouth and shouted down the ravine: "Cattle thief, it's time to come to the Council Rock!"

After a long time they heard the drawling, sleepy snarl of a full-fed tiger. Immediately, Akela gave a bloodcurdling howl and the buffaloes pitched down the slope. Once they had started, there was no way they could stop.

Shere Khan heard the thunder of their hooves and lumbered down the ravine looking for a way to escape, but the sides were too steep. Then he heard the bellow of the cows with their calves in front of him and turned back to face the stampeding bulls. Rama tripped, stumbled and went on again over something soft. With the bulls at his heels he crashed into the other herd, the weight of the charge carrying them all down the ravine and out onto the plain.

Behind them, Shere Khan lay dead.

Shere Khan turned to face the stampeding bulls.

Meanwhile, the herd children had run home to tell how the buffaloes had stampeded. Buldeo strode out to scold Mowgli for not taking better care of the herd. He found him slashing and pulling at Shere Khan's skin, watched by two wolves.

Unlike Buldeo, Mowgli is not interested in money. His idea of a reward is to fulfill his promise to the jungle animals.

"What do you think you're doing? A child can't skin a tiger!" he said angrily. "It's the lame tiger, too. In that case, I'll ignore the fact that you let the herd run off. I might even give you one rupee of the reward when I take the skin to the police."

"So," said Mowgli, "you think you're going to take the hide, claim the reward and give me one rupee? You're wrong, old man. I need the skin for my own use."

"How dare you speak like this to the chief hunter of the village? It's only by sheer luck and the stupidity of the buffaloes that you made this kill. Well, beggar brat, you won't get any of the reward, just a big beating. Now leave the skin alone."

"Akela," muttered Mowgli. "This man is annoying me."

Buldeo suddenly found himself sprawling on the grass with a gray wolf standing over him.

"You're right," continued Mowgli. "I won't get any of the reward, but neither will you. There is an old war between this tiger and myself – and I have won it."

Buldeo found himself sprawling on the grass.

Buldeo lay still on the ground, his head full of wonder at the terrible magic he was witnessing. A wolf that obeyed the orders of a boy who had private wars with man-eating tigers? At any moment he expected Mowgli to turn into a tiger, too.

"Great King," he whispered. "May I get up and go away, or is your servant going to tear me into pieces?"

"Go, and peace go with you. But next time don't meddle with my game," said Mowgli, as he triumphantly pulled Shere Khan's skin clear of the body.

Buldeo hobbled away to the village as fast as he could and told a tale of magic and enchantment and sorcery that concerned the priest greatly.

A few hours later, Mowgli and Akela led the buffaloes back to the village. As they approached, they heard the bells in the temple banging, and when they drew closer a shower of stones whistled around their ears. The villagers began to shout: "Sorcerer! Wolf's brat! Jungle demon! Go away!"

"They're rather like the Pack, these brothers of yours," said Akela. "They seem to want to cast you out."

"Wolf! Wolf's cub! Go away!" shouted the priest.

The villagers began to shout: "Sorcerer! Wolf's brat! Go away!"

"Again?" said Mowgli. "Last time it was because I was a man. This time it's because I'm a wolf. Let's go, Akela."

He turned and walked away with the Lone Wolf. As he looked up at the sky he felt happy. "No more sleeping under a roof for me, Akela. Let's fetch Shere Khan's hide and go home."

When the moon rose over the plain, the horrified villagers watched Mowgli, with two wolves at his heels and a bundle over his head, trotting into the distance. Then they banged the temple bells louder than ever. Messua wept, while Buldeo added more and more details to the story of his adventures in the jungle, till he ended up by saying that Akela had stood up on his hind legs and talked like a man.

The moon was just going down again when Mowgli and the two wolves reached the hill of the Council Rock and stopped at Mother Wolf's cave.

"They have cast me out from the man pack, Mother," shouted Mowgli, "but I have brought Shere Khan's hide, just as I promised."

Mother Wolf walked stiffly from the cave, followed by the cubs. When she saw the skin her eyes glowed.

"It's just as I told him all those years ago, when he crammed his head and shoulders into this cave, hunting for your life, little frog – I told him that the hunter would be hunted. You have done well."

"Little Brother, you have done well," came a deep voice from the thicket. "We were lonely in the jungle without you." Bagheera came running to Mowgli's bare feet and

Mowgli can return to his beloved jungle home once more. But this time he must face the jungle's dangers alone – without a community to protect him.

they clambered up the Council Rock together. Mowgli spread the skin out on the flat stone where Akela used to sit. Akela lay down on it and called, "Look, look well, O Wolves," just as he had when Mowgli was first brought there as a baby.

No one had replaced Akela as leader of the Pack. The wolves had pleased themselves as to when they hunted and fought. But they answered Akela's call from habit. They gathered together on the Council Rock, some of them limping from shot wounds, some lame from traps, some mangy from eating bad food. Many were missing, but those that were left saw Shere Khan's striped hide stretched out on the rock, the huge claws dangling at the end of the empty dangling feet.

"Look well, O Wolves. Have I kept my promise?" said Mowgli. The wolves bayed yes, and one tattered wolf howled:

"Lead us again, Akela. Lead us again, man-cub. We are tired of having no laws to follow. We want to be the Free People once more".

"That cannot be," purred Bagheera. "When you are no longer hungry, you may change your mind again. You are not called the Free People for nothing. You fought for freedom, and it is yours. Eat it then, O Wolves."

"I have been cast out by the man pack and the wolf pack," said Mowgli. "From now onward, I will hunt alone." ☀

"Look well, O Wolves.
Have I kept my promise?"
said Mowgli.

Kipling's Jungle

THE STORIES IN *The Jungle Book* are loved by children throughout the world. As Mowgli the man-cub stumbles into the wolf pack, Kipling takes his readers into the heart of the jungle and reveals the fears and excitements of the animal kingdom.

☀ JUNGLE INSPIRATION

Although Kipling did not explore the jungle himself, he was inspired by his father's book, *Beast and Man in India*. In one chapter, Kipling's father illustrates the mischievous nature of monkeys.

☀ CREATURES GREAT AND SMALL

Kipling introduces his readers to all kinds of animals in his other stories in *The Jungle Book*: there is a plucky mongoose called Riki Tiki Tavi, Nag the evil cobra, and Kala Nag the elephant.

Kala Nag in "Toomai of the Elephants."

Riki Tiki Tavi and Nag the cobra, from an early edition of The Jungle Book.

Mowgli, Baloo, and Bagheera in
The Jungle Book *(© Disney, 1967).*

☀ BEAR NECESSITIES

Several movies of *The Jungle Book* have been made, including Walt Disney's much-loved version. In this cartoon, Bagheera, Baloo, and Kaa sing and dance their way through the jungle with Mowgli as their favorite man-cub. The movie was a huge success – Kipling's jungle story captivated the whole world!

☀ MOWGLI'S LESSONS

Mowgli has to learn many hard lessons in the jungle. To survive, he has to change from a helpless baby into a strong boy. But as his teacher, Baloo, realizes, Mowgli must also learn a more subtle lesson – how to communicate with all the animals in the jungle world.

Inga Moore's illustration of Mowgli and Bagheera in The Jungle Book *(1992).*

☀ MASTER OF THE JUNGLE

The hardest lesson Mowgli has to learn is that he is a man, not an animal. Mowgli learns to accept the responsibilities of adulthood and finally realizes that he is different from the jungle animals.

About the Author

*Rudyard Kipling
(1865–1936)*

RUDYARD KIPLING (1865–1936) was born in Bombay, India. At the age of six, he was sent away from his parents to a school in England, and for many years he was very unhappy. Kipling's love for India stayed with him throughout his childhood, and he started to write poems and short stories inspired by his earliest memories.

The cover of Kipling's book In Black and White.

❋ HOME AGAIN

Kipling returned to India in 1881, and worked as a journalist in Lahore (now in Pakistan). He began to publish poems and stories, and by the early 1890s he was a literary celebrity both in India and in England.

A bookplate illustrated by Kipling in 1902.

Illustrations from Just So Stories, *1902.*

❋ FAME AND FORTUNE

In 1892, Kipling married and moved with his wife to Vermont, where he wrote *The Jungle Book* (1894). By 1897, Kipling had moved back to England with his family. He published his novel *Kim* in 1901 and the much-loved *Just So Stories* in 1902. Five years later, Kipling became the first English writer to be awarded the Nobel Prize for Literature.

Kipling's study in his home in Sussex, England.